PAINTBALL
BOSS

BY JAKE MADDOX

text by
Tyler Omoth

STONE ARCH BOOKS
a capstone imprint

Jake Maddox JV books are published by Stone Arch Books
A Capstone Imprint
1710 Roe Crest Drive
North Mankato, Minnesota 56003
www.mycapstone.com

Library of Congress Cataloging-in-Publication Data is available on the
Library of Congress website

ISBN: 978-1-4965-3982-3 (hardcover) 978-1-4965-3986-1 (paperback)
978-1-4965-3990-8 (ebook PDF)

Summary: Quinton, commander of his paintball team, hopes to beat a rival team in the
tournament, but is disappointed that one of his teammates seems to be slowing the team
down — that is, until Quinton finds out what being a commander is really about and learns
to do the right thing, no matter what the cost.

Art Director: Nathan Gassman
Designer: Sarah Bennett
Production Specialist: Katy LaVigne

Photo Credits:
Shutterstock: Aaron Amat, design element, Brocreative, design element, DeanHarty, design
element, Dmitry Kalinovsky, design element, hin255, design element, irin-k, design element,
nikkytok, Cover

J
MADDOX
JAKE

Printed and bound in the United States of America.
009622F16

TABLE OF CONTENTS

CHAPTER 1

PAINTBALL SUMMER

The final excruciating seconds of the school year ticked away. In a few moments, Quinton would be on summer vacation gearing up for his favorite activity in the whole world: the annual paintball tournament. He kept his eyes glued to the clock. He felt like a hawk preparing to take flight. *Four, three, two, one!*

The bell rang, and even the normally proper Ms. Determan smiled. "Ah, the sweet sound of summer! Don't forget your summer reading lists to prepare you for eighth grade. And try to stay out of trouble!"

With a cheer, all of Quinton's classmates snatched up their books and rushed toward the door.

Just a few more days until the paintball tournament! Quinton thought.

As Quinton reached the door, a hard shoulder slammed him into the doorframe.

"Look out, dragon-boy!" said Zach. He sneered as he pushed his way through the other kids in the hall. "Get ready to lose again!"

"Wow, what a jerk!" said a familiar voice behind Quinton.

He knew without even looking that it was Ethan. Quinton turned to see his best friends, Logan and Ethan, standing close by him. Ethan grinned from freckled ear to freckled ear.

"He's just scared," Quinton said, rubbing his shoulder where it had hit the doorframe.

As they started walking, Ethan began to bounce around him and Logan. "This is it! The

Summer Paintball Tournament trophy is ours this time. I can feel it! Even Zach's band of monsters can't stop us, right, Logan?"

Logan smiled. "Yeah. I guess so."

Quinton slapped him on the shoulder. "Come on, man!" he said. "Think about it. With you and Ethan marking people left and right and my skills as commander, The Dragons are a lock to take home the trophy this year. I don't care what Zach thinks. We've been practicing all year. My aim is way better and Ethan is nearly impossible to hit!"

"I am pretty nimble," Ethan said, smiling a crooked smile.

Quinton continued, "You put that together with your timing, Logan, and Danny's rapid-fire shots, and we are the team to beat! We attack hard and fast and together. We are the Dragons!"

The three boys reached their lockers and shoveled a year's worth of books, scraps, and empty soda cans into their backpacks.

Logan shut his locker with a bang. "And Adam," he said.

"What?" Quinton and Ethan asked at the same time.

"I said, 'and Adam,'" Logan said, standing as tall as he could. "I know you think you have this all figured out, but we're a five-person team. You always forget Adam. This isn't just your show, you know."

Ethan rolled his eyes, slung his backpack over his shoulder, and fist-bumped Quinton. "See ya later, bud."

As Ethan ran down the hall, jumping to touch the mascot sign on his way out the door, Quinton slammed his locker and turned to Logan.

"Okay. Sorry, I forgot Adam," Quinton said. "What's your deal? Are you even excited for this season at all?"

Logan sighed. "I don't like you acting like my brother is some sort of afterthought. You never even include him in the game plan. Adam has worked just as hard as any of us and has improved his shooting a lot this year. He would surprise you if you gave him a chance."

Quinton huffed in frustration. "How? He's about half as big as the rest of us, he's not very fast, and when the game starts, he's always hiding! I think I'm a pretty good team commander, but how am I supposed to make use of a player like that?" Quinton shifted on his feet. "You know he's only on the team because your mom brought it up in front of my mom. I didn't really have a choice."

Logan looked at him and sighed. They slung their backpacks over their shoulders and walked toward the door together. The sun was shining brightly as if announcing the beginning of the most beautiful summer yet, but Quinton felt like there was a cloud hanging over them.

Why was Logan being so difficult? They finally had a near-perfect team and they'd practiced really hard all year long. It didn't make sense. He wasn't telling him anything he didn't know.

Logan stopped outside the school doors and turned to Quinton, "Look, maybe Adam wasn't your first choice. But doesn't a good commander make the best possible use of his team's skills?"

"Yeah, but I'm not a magician! Adam doesn't have any paintball skills," Quinton replied. His face was hot now.

Logan glared at him. Quinton glared back. They stood face to face with their hands on their hips like gunfighters from the old West, each waiting for the other to draw first.

"I think you're not trying hard enough. I think we should consider some new strategies," Logan said defiantly. "You're not the only one who knows how to play paintball."

"Why? Why would we try new strategies when ours works? Our team is made to move fast and strike hard." Quinton continued, "Except for

Adam. If he can't handle it, maybe we could let him sit this one out?"

"What are you saying?" Logan asked. "You want to kick my brother off the team?"

"Not permanently or anything. I just really want to win the tournament this year and there are some other guys who don't have teams yet. Just imagine if we had one more athletic, fast guy to complete the swarm!"

Logan adjusted his backpack on his shoulder and spun on his heel toward the door without saying a word. When he got to the door he shoved it so hard it hit the wall with a loud bang.

Quinton knew Logan was really mad but he also knew he'd come to his senses. Quinton yelled after him, "Remember, we have our first scrimmage tomorrow at noon!"

Shaking his head, Quinton hoisted up his own backpack and started his long walk home. He didn't mind the walk. He had a lot to think about.

If he could replace the small and timid Adam with a bigger, faster player, who would he pick? He'd thought about it all year, but now that the thought was out in the open, he could seriously consider other players. Quinton felt a little relieved that he and Logan had talked about this, even if Logan was mad. They'd been friends forever — Quinton knew he'd get over it. Logan wanted to win, too.

He was still running the names of other kids through his head as he reached the front door of his home. Then he heard his phone's text tone. After a little bit of digging through his backpack, he found his phone and checked the new message. It was from Logan.

If Adam is off the team for the tournament, then so am I. We'll be at the scrimmage tomorrow so you have tonight to think about it.

CHAPTER 2

SCRIMMAGE SURPRISE

The next day Quinton leaned against the wall of Splatmasters Paintball Arena, waiting for his team to arrive. They usually met twenty minutes before a scrimmage to get ready. He fidgeted with his duffel bag, checking and double-checking his paintball gear. By 11:40, he saw Ethan and Danny zipping down the street on their bikes toward him.

Okay, he thought, *that's two. I need two more. Logan wouldn't ditch the team already, would he? He said I had the night to think about it.*

"Hey, Q, what's up?" asked Ethan in his usual cheerful way. "Where are Logan and the brat? They're usually the first ones here."

"They'll be here any minute," Quinton said. He hoped he sounded more confident than he felt. He shook off his worry and stepped into commander mode. "We should check our gear while we wait. Just a heads up, guys, I think we're stuck with Adam for the tournament. Without him, we'd lose Logan. We'll all just have to step up our game a little to cover for him."

Ethan and Danny looked at each other and shrugged. Ethan said, "I didn't even know you were thinking about getting rid of Adam. I'd miss the little guy."

Danny said, "Yeah. What's this about?"

But Quinton shook his head, irritated. He figured he must be the only one to see clearly since he was commander. He felt a trickle of doubt, but he shook it off. If he second-guessed himself, his

14

whole strategy might go out the window. That wouldn't be good for anyone.

Just as they were packing their paintball equipment away again, Logan and Adam walked around the corner. It was still only 11:50, so they had time to spare. Quinton exhaled in relief and rushed forward to meet them.

"Hey," Quinton said, looking first at Logan and then at Adam.

"Hey," Logan replied.

"I thought about what you said, and yeah. We're too good to mess up this team now."

"The *whole* team?" Logan asked. He put his arm around his little brother's shoulders.

"The whole team, as it is," Quinton replied.

Adam said, "I won't let you down, you know."

Quinton wasn't so sure, but he nodded anyway. He turned and the three of them walked over to Ethan and Danny, who were still waiting. Quinton surveyed his team: The Dragons were ready for summer and their first scrimmage. Even if it wasn't the exact team Quinton had hoped for.

Once the teams were geared up, the officials announced the pairings. The Dragons were scrimmaging against the Paint Bandits.

Quinton knew this team shouldn't be a problem for them. Still, it was a good test to see how far they had come since last summer. They had worked on their individual skills and even had some scrimmages across town against older teams during the off-season. But summer was when the real games began. It was time to see if they were ready to start winning.

"Okay, guys," Quinton said. "You all know your parts, right? Logan and I will charge, and Ethan and Danny will alternate with us. If you're not moving, provide cover fire. Adam, you hang back a little and watch for sneak attacks from either flank. Just yell out if you see anyone. This team usually lets the paintballs fly in the first volley and then hangs back. They're not very organized. Let's do this!"

This was a team death match, so the first team to mark all of the other team's players was the winner. Quinton looked over the Dragons — everyone was ready. Just before the official blew the air horn to mark the start of the match, he saw Logan lean over and whisper something to Adam and point to a position on the field. Quinton knew that the Paint Bandits liked to shoot early, but would duck for cover after the first volley of fire. That worked right into his strategy. He hoped Logan was telling Adam to play it safe and go hide.

When the sound of the air horn filled the air, Danny and Ethan sprinted forward, taking cover behind two bunkers in the middle of the field, ducking and dodging a barrage of red paintballs that flew through the air. Quinton and Logan stayed slightly behind, choosing cover behind the closest bunkers. No one was hit.

Quinton peered around the edge of his bunker and signaled Danny. With a nod, Danny and Ethan dropped to the ground so they could see forward. As practiced, they started shooting wildly. This made the Paint Bandits dive for cover as Quinton and Logan charged forward, protected by their teammate's rapid fire. As they charged, they zigged and zagged, constantly looking for the other team's players.

Quinton surprised one player, marking him squarely on the shoulder. Then he got another one whose leg was sticking out. The players called out, "I'm marked!" as soon as the paintballs hit them.

Danny took out a third player and whooped with excitement, but Ethan took a paintball to the arm as he tried to move to a better vantage point.

Quinton loved a fast start to a game. The Dragons were already up 3–1. He turned to look at Logan, but suddenly realized he wasn't in sight anymore.

Where did he go? He wasn't sticking to the plan.

The sound of markers firing and paintballs splattering off to the right side of the arena made Quinton sprint for a strategic spot on that side. But as soon as he got there, someone called out, "I'm marked!" About two seconds later it was followed by, "Me, too. I'm out!"

At that moment, the loudspeaker crackled and the referee's voice called out. "That's the match! The Dragons win 5–1. Nice game, guys."

* * *

After the match, the team went over to the cafeteria. It was team tradition to celebrate a victory with a soda and a quick recap.

"Nice game, guys," said Ethan. "Sorry I got marked before I could get anyone. It was a reckless move."

"Hey, it happens," Quinton replied. "We won. That's what matters."

"How many did you mark? I got one," asked Danny.

"I marked two," Quinton said, grinning.

They all turned to look at Logan.

"I didn't hit anybody," he said.

All at once Danny, Ethan, and Quinton turned in their seats and looked at Adam. Logan patted him on the back and Adam held up two fingers. He smiled shyly.

"Atta boy!" hooted Ethan.

"Nice going," added Danny.

"Thanks, guys," Adam said with a shrug. "I've been working on my shooting."

Quinton could feel his face getting hot. Adam had done well, but he and Logan had made their own plays — like Quinton, as commander, didn't even matter. Teams fell apart when they didn't stick together.

Quinton stood up and looked at Logan. "What were you saying to Adam before the match?

Whatever you guys did, it wasn't part of the strategy I laid out. What's the deal?"

Logan shrugged. "I wanted to try something."

"Whatever it was, it must have worked!" Danny said. He and Ethan slapped a high five.

Quinton swallowed down his anger. "Well, are you going to tell us or keep it a big secret?"

"Tomorrow," Logan replied. "I call a team meeting. Wilson's Woods at ten a.m. The usual place."

"You're calling team meetings now?" Quinton crossed his arms over his chest. What was happening? He felt like he was in one of those stories where a ship's captain is overthrown by his sailors. It made him feel panicky, like no one respected him anymore. Especially his best friend.

"I'm sorry," Logan said, "are you the only one allowed to do that, too?"

Quinton looked around and saw confused faces. Evidently, he was the only one upset about this. He could tell that the others wanted to hear what Logan had to say, so he tried to shake off his frustration. "No, I guess not. It's fine by me." He shrugged and looked away.

Everyone agreed that they could make it and started for the door as they slurped up the last of their sodas.

As he rode his bike home, Quinton thought, *Logan and I have been best friends for years. This isn't like him. This wouldn't be happening if we hadn't been forced to put Adam on the team.*

CHAPTER 3

MUTINY IN THE WOODS

Quinton reached the meeting spot in the woods first. It wasn't much of a meeting spot, really. There wasn't a table or snack bar or anything. It was just a spot where two trees had fallen over during a summer storm years ago. Those tree trunks were just the right height for sitting on. Quinton couldn't help but smile as he made his way through the woods. Many of the trees had blotches of colors on their trunks and leaves. It sort of looked like the trees had the measles. Those blotches were from hours and hours of practice the

Dragons had put in over the last year. Paintball out in the woods, or woodsball, made them sharper in other venues.

When he reached the meeting spot, he tossed his backpack on the ground and jumped up on one of the tree trunks to wait. After a few minutes, Logan and Adam arrived, followed by Ethan and Danny moments later. Once everyone was settled in, an awkward silence fell over the team. The only sound was a nearby squirrel that seemed agitated to have five kids disrupting its day.

They all looked at Quinton expectantly. He shrugged. "Don't look at me," he said. "I didn't call this meeting. This is Logan's show."

As they turned toward Logan, Ethan piped up. "What did you guys do during yesterday's match? I never saw either of you after the start."

Logan smiled and Adam grinned. "That's the point," Logan said, "You're not supposed to see us. Well, Adam anyway. Right, little bro?"

"Yep," Adam said. "I hid right away."

"That's nothing new," Danny said. He looked directly at Adam. "It's smart to find cover, but it's hard to take out players if you only hide. And eventually you'll be found and marked."

"Yeah," Logan continued, "you might think so, but while you guys were running around like crazy, we had a plan. I bolted from bunker to bunker, just slow enough for them to see me, but leading them over to the far right side of the playing field. And just when they thought they had me . . ."

"Adam marked them from his hiding spot," Quinton finished for him. "So what?" He shifted on the log.

"So, I'm proposing that we change our strategy. We don't need to charge recklessly at the other team. We can lure them into traps and take them out," Logan finished.

"But we've never played that way. I've never seen a team play that way," Ethan said.

"Exactly," said Adam. He smiled.

Quinton could see that the team was thinking about this, about overriding his careful strategies. Irritation prickled through him. "Are you serious? We're the Dragons! We swoop in, use our strength and skill, and take out the other team. It's how we've always done it and it works! This year we're bigger and faster than ever. Adam is small enough to hide — I'll give you that. But how do we know he didn't just get lucky in the scrimmage?" Quinton plopped back down on his log in frustration.

"How often do you watch Adam when we practice?" Logan asked.

"He doesn't," Adam chimed in. "He thinks I'm no good."

"I focus on what we do best! And . . . ," Quinton sighed. "I'm sorry, Adam, but you're not as fast or athletic as the rest of us."

"But now he's the best marksman on the team," Logan said. "By far."

"Oh, he is?" Quinton smiled. Now he had them where he wanted them. They were bragging and he could put an end to all of this. "Can he prove it?"

"Ah! I was hoping you'd ask that," Logan said. He reached into his backpack, pulled out a tin can, and handed it to Adam. Adam ran into the woods and put the can on top of a tree stump about 20 yards away.

"Who thinks they can hit that from here?" Logan asked.

"I do," Quinton said.

"Me too," said Danny.

Ethan nodded. "Yep."

"Great. Here's Adam's marker. Give it your best shot." Logan handed the marker to Quinton.

Quinton raised the marker and took aim. He fired at the can. *Thwack!* A bright yellow paint blotch plastered the stump two feet below the target. He tried again, but this time the paintball sailed over the can and landed harmlessly in the leaves behind it.

Danny pelted the stump with his shot and Ethan missed badly.

"That's why we shoot sprays of three pellets at a time," said Ethan. "These markers are the only ones legal for tournament play, but they're not very accurate at all."

Logan stood up. "Show them how it's done, Adam."

Adam took his marker back from Ethan and then knelt down on one knee. He rested one elbow on his knee while he aimed. *Ping!* With a splash of yellow, the can somersaulted off of the stump.

"Wow!" said Danny

"Nice shot!" Ethan echoed.

Quinton rolled his eyes. "Okay, so he got better at shooting. That doesn't change anything. We're still the strongest team out there. This doesn't mean we should change *everything*. Especially since it's working and we have a shot at winning this year."

"I think we should vote on it," Logan said. "Instead of attacking like dragons, we can set traps like spiders and lure them in!"

"Adopt your new style or keep playing the way we know?" Quinton asked. "And if your spider-style doesn't win this vote, you'll keep playing my way?"

"Fine."

"Okay, let's vote. Who wants to keep playing Dragon-style, attacking our opponents?" Quinton raised his hand and looked at the others.

Ethan and Danny glanced at each other and then slowly raised their hands.

"There you have it," Quinton said. "Now we can focus on the tournament."

"Okay," Logan said. His shoulders slumped a little. "If that's what you guys want."

"Sorry, Logan," Danny said.

"My mom always says don't fix something if it isn't broken," Ethan said. Then he winked at Adam. "Heckuva shot, though, Adam."

Adam looked at his brother. Quinton could see frustration radiating from him. For a moment, he felt bad.

"Maybe not this time, Adam," Logan said, "but don't worry. You'll get your shot."

Adam shrugged and looked at the ground. Quinton felt a pang of guilt but he shook it off.

"The tournament announcement is tomorrow, so let's all meet at the snack bar at eleven. I've heard there is an extra special twist this year, so let's be ready for anything," Quinton said. "Who's going to win this year?"

"The Dragons! The Dragons! The Dragons!"

Quinton noticed that Logan and Adam joined in the cheer, even though they looked disappointed.

Good, he thought, *he's not going to be a sore loser. Zach's team, our biggest competition, is ready to compete, and Logan tries to change our whole style right before the tournament! If only we could replace Adam with someone faster.*

CHAPTER 4

BIG NEWS

Quinton slurped on a flavored ice while the team waited for Bob, the owner of Splatmasters Arena, to kick off the tournament with his announcements. Most of it was the same every year. Eight teams per division, standard rules applied, and then a long speech about safety. Quinton didn't mind, though. He'd once taken a paintball right in his face mask. He probably would be blind in one eye if he hadn't been wearing his goggles. He maybe wouldn't even have that eye anymore. Besides, safety equipment didn't really slow you down.

The exciting part was the twist. Each year the tournament judges added an interesting twist. One year everyone had to wear moon boots, which was really weird. The next year it was a capture the flag competition instead of a standard team death match.

"What do you think the catch will be this year, Commander Quinton?" Ethan grinned as he guzzled a giant soda.

"I don't know," Quinton replied.

"Maybe they'll make each team swap a player," Danny offered, "or make us all wear the same color shirts and pants!"

Quinton stood up. "Huddle up, Dragons!" he said. "Whatever they announce, remember how we play. We attack and we swarm. There's no wrinkle they can add that would ruin our strategy. This is our year!"

"Hoorah, Dragons!" they all yelled together.

An air horn blew and they knew it was time for Bob to make the announcement. They all turned to look at the podium. What they saw surprised them all. Bob was standing behind the podium holding his usual bullhorn to make the announcements. But he wasn't dressed like he normally was. Today, he was wearing a camouflage outfit and had grown a scraggly beard. The kids all laughed.

"Nice beard, Bob!" one kid yelled.

"Did you sleep in the woods this winter?" another kid shouted.

With a smile, Bob raised one hand to quiet his good-natured hecklers. After a couple of squeals and squawks from the bullhorn, he addressed the crowd. "All right, all right. Take your shots." He winked at a group of kids who were still snickering. "I guess you guys have never seen me during hunting season, huh? But that's what we have here, folks. It's time for the Eighth Annual

Summer Paintball Tournament and this year's theme is 'Take to the Woods'!"

Quinton and Logan stared at each other excitedly before slapping a high five. Woodsball was right up their alley. Their entire practice field was in the woods! The only thing that could make this better would be if . . .

"That's right," Bob continued. "This year's tournament will be played out at Wilson's Woods, just a few blocks away!"

This time the whole team whooped in delight. They knew every hill and dip of those woods. They knew which trees were big enough to hide behind. There was no way they could lose now!

"But that's not all!" said Bob. The kids hushed, eager to hear what else he would say. "I'm proud to announce that this year's tournament has a new sponsor: Larry's Sporting Goods and Paintball Emporium. Not only have they donated money to help us hire referees and provide refreshments for the tournament, but they've also provided a $100 gift card to their store."

Bob went on, "The winning team will get the standard free admission to Splatmasters Arena. And, for the first year ever, the Annual Summer Paintball Tournament will be awarding an individual Most Valuable Player, who will receive the gift card as a prize. MVP will be determined by the total number of marks a player has at the end of the tournament."

The announcement created a major buzz of excited conversation. An MVP! Immediately Quinton thought of a handful of players who he considered to be the best players in town. He put himself at the top of that list. Logan and Zach were two others. But with the tournament going to Wilson's Woods, he realized that he and Logan easily had the best shot at taking the trophy. One hundred dollars! That would buy one seriously awesome marker, or a lot of other supplies.

"Whoa! Did you hear that?" Ethan bounced around excitedly. "Woodsball and an MVP this year! One of us is going to take home that prize."

"Hey Logan, who do you think has a better shot, you or Quinton?" Danny asked.

"I don't know. Zach has some pretty good players on his team, too. And The Dragons have a whole team of good players. It's anybody's game," Logan said.

Quinton didn't say anything. He wasn't sure the Dragons had a *whole* team of good players. *Hmm,* he thought. *Maybe I could find a way to make Adam's skill fit the team better. But how?*

Before he could come up with an idea, he heard Zach's voice right behind him.

"Nice of them to create an MVP award for me, don't you think?" he said.

"MVP doesn't stand for Most *Vile* Person, Zach," Ethan said.

"Yeah," said Danny. "We have a couple of contenders on our team, too!"

"Who?" Zach sneered. "You've all got the same shot at it as Adam. And by that, I mean no shot at all. You may as well all just go and hide!"

Ethan and Danny started to open their mouths, but Logan put his hands on their shoulders and pulled them away. "Come on, guys. Don't let him get you riled. We need to focus."

They walked away from Zach as he and his team snickered.

"I can't stand that guy," Danny muttered.

"Okay guys, huddle up!" Quinton said. "The tournament starts tomorrow and we have no idea which team we'll be facing. When you get home, check your equipment and make sure everything is in shape. I know we can win it all this year, especially in Wilson's Woods!"

"Yeah!" they all shouted together. "Go Dragons!"

As he watched them turn to leave, Quinton grabbed Logan's arm. "You have a sec?"

"Sure, what's up?"

"I'm sorry things didn't go your way at the meeting, but I thought maybe you could help me figure out a way to make Adam's marksmanship work with our swarming style," Quinton said.

"I've been thinking about that. If he can find a high vantage point, he could provide some cover fire as we move forward."

"That's a good idea," Quinton said. "Thanks."

Quinton was happy to hear that Logan had been thinking about it, but he was still worried. Would Logan and Adam play with the team, or would they ignore Quinton's strategy again?

CHAPTER 5

SHOTS FIRED

By the time Quinton reached the snack bar the next morning, the rest of the team was already there, dressed and ready for the match. They each wore a crimson red T-shirt that read "The Dragons." Logan and Adam's mom had had them made for the whole team. Though the T-shirts were mostly covered by protective gear, Quinton thought the team looked fierce in them. As he approached the table, Adam jumped up and handed him a sheet of paper.

"This is the schedule?" Quinton asked. His hands were shaking as he tried to read it. Was he nervous or excited? He couldn't tell.

"Yep," Adam replied. "We're up first against the Spray Painters."

On the bus that took the teams from the paintball arena to Wilson's Woods, Quinton looked over the tournament bracket. "Good," he said. "We don't match up against Zach unless we meet in the finals. Which means we should definitely make it to the finals. Let's go get these guys and win!"

* * *

Just before the starting horn went off, Quinton saw Logan talking to Adam again. After a pat on Adam's helmet, Logan took his position. Even though Quinton was worried they were talking about different strategies again, he grinned at his buddy. The tournament was about to start in Wilson's Woods, where he and Logan had played for years! This was going to be fun.

The rest of the Dragons took their starting positions. The other teams lined up around the teams playing the match to view the start of the action. They wouldn't be able to see much during the match, but they could see the beginning.

The blare of an air horn shook the leaves on the trees and sent birds scattering for safety. The game was on! Just like in the scrimmage, Danny and Ethan rushed ahead to find sheltered spots, only this time behind trees instead of bunkers. Quinton and Logan took up spots behind them and prepared to move forward. Out of the corner of his eye, Quinton saw Adam dash off to the right behind some trees. *Oh, great.* Quinton thought. *He's running to hide again.*

Then he saw Adam come out from the trees and dive down behind a stump at the top of a small rise — a perfect spot to provide cover fire.

Quinton met Logan's gaze and bobbed his head, counting to three. On the third nod, they took off as the rest of the team filled the air ahead of them with whizzing paintballs. As the other team dove for cover, the Dragons took note of their positions. Quinton dashed to the left and marked two players who were trying to hide behind trees that were too thin. He marked another one as he tried to dive in a bush for cover.

He could tell by the cries of "I'm marked!" that the game was going quickly. He looked around for Logan. As he ran around a bank of bushes, Quinton felt a paintball peg him in the left shoulder. They were only paintballs, but they hurt a little when they hit. After wincing for just a second, he let out a yell. "I'm marked!"

When he reached the dead box, he saw that Danny was already there, but also that four of the other team's five players were already marked too. It only took a minute for the last player on the Spray Painters to call out, and the match was over. The Dragons had won this one easily.

The teams both reunited in the common area outside of the woods and reported to the officials. All the teams in the tournament gathered around.

"Congratulations to the Dragons on the first victory of this year's tournament!" Bob called out. "Your top scorer is Quinton, with three marks!"

"All right!" someone in the crowd cheered.

"Way to go, Big Q!" another voice called out.

Quinton grinned and relished the cheers. His joy was short-lived, however, as he saw Zach pushing kids aside, stomping toward him.

"Good game, dragon-boy," Zach said with a sneer. "But don't start thinking you have a shot at the MVP award. We were watching and we have you figured out. Besides, I thought you would have gotten a little better over the last year. Did you even practice at all?"

"Shut up, Zacharias!" Ethan said. For a rare moment, Ethan wasn't smiling. Quinton knew that was serious.

"Ooh, big talker. At least I see you finally found a use for your little guy. Perched him on a hill, huh?" Zach jerked his thumb to the right, pointing at Adam. "I guess when you're carrying a little dead weight, you want to at least give him a good view of the action!"

Zach's teammates erupted into laughter. Quinton couldn't stand Zach's smugness, but he secretly agreed. Could they have done even better with a different fifth player?

"You tell 'em, Zach!"

Zach turned and gave fist-bumps all around to his teammates.

Splat!

"Oww!" Zach yelped as he grabbed his backside, now covered in yellow paint. "Who shot me?"

The whole crowd looked around. Before long all eyes landed on Danny. He stood motionless, holding his marker in front of him and wearing a big grin.

"Adam is our teammate, not 'dead weight,' yellow pants," he said calmly to Zach.

"Why, you little . . ." Zach said.

The crowd roared with laughter, but it was cut short by Bob's air horn blast. Quinton groaned. He knew what was coming. How could Danny do this to them?

"Danny!" he said, shaking his head.

Bob turned to announce to all the teams, "Danny is suspended for one game. The Dragons may not substitute."

Quinton saw Logan reach over and pat Danny on the back. "Thanks, man," he said.

"Sorry, kid," Bob said quietly. Then, using the bullhorn, he announced the next match. "Up next, Zach's Bunker Bashers versus the Splatballers!"

"Come on, Bashers," Zach yelled. "Let's show these losers how it's done!"

As the teams all took their places either to play or to watch, Quinton walked over to Danny.

"Why did you do that?" he asked. "Now we're going to have to play short in the next round!"

Danny shrugged. "I didn't like him bashing my teammate. Besides, you won't need me. Heck, I didn't score a mark in today's match, anyway."

"You didn't?"

"Nope."

"I had three," Quinton said, " which means two others probably had one each. Logan and Ethan?"

Logan grinned. "No, bro. That would be two for Adam."

The team turned to see Adam lift his marker and blow on the tip as if it were a smoking gun. He said, "One mark right away. And then the other player at 25 yards just after he marked Quinton."

CHAPTER 6

THE DRAGONS DECIDE

Bob's air horn blasted its call into the woods to signal the beginning of the second match. Quinton and the rest of the Dragons were standing at a good vantage point in the observation area and anxious to see what Zach's team could do. While they couldn't afford to overlook any team, his Bunker Busters were last year's winners and considered the favorite to win again this year. The most interesting part was that they used a style similar to the Dragons: a fast-paced swarming attack.

At the sound of the horn, the team opposing Zach's Bunker Busters scattered wide, left and right.

"Look at that!" Logan said, pointing at the team's technique.

"What are they doing?" asked Ethan.

"Trying to confuse Zach's squad," Logan said.

"Well," Danny said, "it's not working."

Quinton watched Zach's team move forward with a speed and agility he'd never seen before. As two players raced forward, three players covered. When they saw the other team's split maneuver, Zach signaled his team to follow him, and they all swerved to the right, continuing their advance.

"Oh, man," Logan said. "They are toast!"

To confuse Zach's team, their opponents had split up into two smaller squads. Zach, not taking the bait, had his whole team follow the smaller squad. In a flurry of paintballs and pops, Zach's Bunker Busters took them out.

Only one of Zach's players was hit. The rest of the team turned to pursue the other squad and at that point the match was practically a squirrel hunt in the woods. The other team obviously wasn't prepared for Zach's team to react so quickly and not to split up.

In a matter of minutes, the game was over.

"Gather 'round!" Bob yelled out. "Zach's Bunker Busters wins the match by a score of 5–1. Zach is the lead scorer with two marks. Well done, boys! Keep checking the bracket on the concession stand wall to see when you play next. There are two more matches today."

The Dragons stuck around to watch the remaining matches, taking note of how each team played. Were they fast? Were they aggressive? How well did they communicate? Just as Quinton had expected, the other teams were okay, but he didn't think any of them could challenge the Dragons or Zach's Bunker Busters.

Of course, that was when they hadhad a full team. Thanks to Danny's hotheaded move, they had to play the next match shorthanded. Even a mediocre team would be dangerous with numbers in their favor.

After the final match, the team met back at the snack bar to talk about the action of the day.

"The teams all look better this year," said Ethan. "I guess we weren't the only ones working on our game during the off-season."

"Yeah, maybe," Quinton said, "but we're still the team to beat."

"If we can win one short-handed," Logan said.

Everyone looked at Danny.

"Sorry, guys," he said. "I couldn't help myself."

"I know it put us in a hard spot," Logan said, "but I loved it! Did you see Zach's face when that paintball hit him?"

Ethan mimicked a pained expression with crossed eyes, and everyone laughed for a bit.

"All right," Quinton said, "even I have to admit that it was funny, but it was against the rules and we're paying for it now. Danny's temper has put us in a tough spot. It's not going to be easy to take down a full team when we start with only four, so we'll have to really stay focused and move fast!"

"Or . . . ," Logan began, "this could be the perfect time to try a new strategy."

"Not this again," Quinton said, rolling his eyes. He felt that now-familiar clenching in his stomach. "We've already voted on how we play."

"Things have changed," Logan said, "and a good commander can change with the scenario. Think about it. Adam is small enough to hide effectively, and he's a dead shot. If we coordinate our movements to lead the other team to him, he can pick them off one by one."

"Maybe it's worth a try," Ethan said.

"What?" Quinton couldn't believe what he was hearing. "Now you're on his side too?"

"I'm just saying that it might be interesting to switch things up a little," Ethan explained. "No other team here plays like that. Even our team has played the same style for the last couple of years. If we mix it up, we might just catch them off guard."

"I think it would help even the odds," Logan added. "But, we'd need to practice so we know what we're doing."

"There's a stump on the right side that has some bushes behind it," Adam chimed in. "If I can get to it, I could hide there easily."

Quinton slammed his hand down on the table, startling everyone, including himself. "No! That won't work!" he said. "Here's how we're going to do it. We are the Dragons. We come in hard and fast and keep moving so they can't hit us. Adam will find a vantage point and see if he can snipe one or two from there."

"But . . . ," Ethan began.

"No! No buts!" Quinton said. "This is *my* team. I started it. I picked you guys two years ago and now we have a chance to win the tournament, but we're going to do it my way!" Quinton picked up his gear bag, slung it over his shoulder, and turned to stalk away.

"Quinton!" Logan yelled after him. "You need to chill out! It's just paintball."

Quinton kept walking, rubbing his hand. It hurt a little. He hadn't meant to react that way, but he'd worked hard to come up with a winning strategy and now it felt like everyone was turning against him.

Just then, his cell phone buzzed. It was a text from Logan. *Just trying to win. Nothing personal. We're with you. We'll get them tomorrow.*

CHAPTER 7

SHORTHANDED SURPRISE

The next morning the team met at the usual spot, geared up and ready to go in the second round of the tournament. They all looked ready for the match, but no one was talking to each other as they normally would. Quinton wondered if they really planned on sticking to the strategy, or if they'd turn against him. He figured there was no way to really know, so he'd just have to trust them.

"Hey, guys," he said, "are we all ready? This team is pretty good and plays in a similar style to ours, so be ready for the paint to fly."

"Whatever you say, Commander," Adam said.

Quinton looked at him, trying to figure out if Adam was sincere or trying to mock him. He seemed sincere.

"Yep, we're good," Ethan said. His typical grin held a hint of nervousness. "Locked and loaded."

"Go get 'em, guys," Danny said. "Sorry I won't be out there with you."

Logan patted him on the back. "We'll win this one for you. Just don't mark anyone in the gallery while we're playing!" The team laughed, and Quinton could almost feel the tension in the air relax a bit. They were ready.

They walked together to their starting point. Each teammate took a turn fist-bumping Danny before he walked over to his starting position in the dead box.

"Today's first match is the Dragons against the Sharks!" Bob announced. "The Dragons must start with one player in the dead box as a penalty for his hair trigger outside the area of play." Everyone laughed except Zach, who crossed his arms and scowled.

Quinton smiled. Zach loved making fun of other kids but obviously didn't like being on the receiving end of the joke himself.

Bob raised his air horn. "Everyone set?" He paused and looked over both teams. With a slight nod of his head, he pressed down on the button and the air horn blasted out the start of round two.

Just like last time, Adam split off to find a good vantage point to provide cover fire. Quinton, Logan, and Ethan ran forward toward the other team. Instead of charging forward two by two, they took turns, with one person advancing while the other two provided cover fire. Quinton noticed that the other team was charging in similar fashion, so the two teams would likely meet in the middle of the woods for a free-for-all. The other team was moving as fast, if not even faster than, the

Dragons. He had to admit, it seemed like everyone had improved a lot since last year.

Suddenly, Quinton heard someone yell, "I'm marked!" It was someone from the other team. *Good. We've evened the numbers.* As they neared the middle of the woods, Ethan took his turn charging forward as Logan and Quinton watched for opponents. As Ethan ran to his new spot, a blast of orange paint exploded on his back, knocking him to the ground.

"Ouch! Oh, man, I'm marked!" he cried out.

So much for even numbers.

Quinton motioned for Logan to come to his side. The Sharks would expect players to come straight at them, but if Quinton and Logan could swing around and both attack from one side, they may be able to surprise them.

Logan nodded and sprinted to Quinton's side. Running as fast as they could, they took off for the left side of the woods. When they reached the edge, they advanced toward their opponents from the side. They found two players hiding behind a pair of oak trees, but they were looking the wrong way. Quinton and Logan opened fire and immediately marked one of them in the shoulder. The other one spun around and fired back — but too late. They'd marked him. Two more down. But before Quinton could celebrate, one of the paintballs the player had fired exploded on his shoulder.

"I'm marked!" he yelled. *Oh, no*, he thought. *It's two on two now, but Logan only has Adam for a partner. We're going to lose!*

Quinton made his way to the dead box and then tried to find the best position to see the playing field. Logan retreated and ran hard from tree to tree, avoiding the other team. Quinton couldn't figure out what he was doing.

"Where is he going?" Quinton asked.

"Where do you think?" Danny responded.

"He's going to find his marksman brother. It's his game now."

Logan kept dodging from tree to tree until he was close to where Adam was hiding. Quinton saw them look at each other and nod. With a *pop*, a paintball blasted into the tree that was shielding Logan and two more paintballs whizzed by to land harmlessly in the leaves. Logan drew a deep breath and ran toward Adam, leaping over the log and stopping behind an oak tree a few feet away. His pursuer broke cover, running toward his new hiding spot. He never made it. *Pop! Pop!* Adam put two paintballs right on his midsection.

"I'm marked!" the boy cried out. He was shaking his head and looking around to see where the shots had come from, but couldn't see Adam's hiding spot.

One down, one to go! Quinton thought.

Logan ran from tree to tree again, looking for the last remaining opponent. When he found him, he backtracked toward Adam again. As he ducked and ran from a giant maple tree to another oak, a blast of orange paint splattered on his leg, tripping him. When Logan fell, he was only a few feet from where Adam was hiding.

"I'm marked!" Logan said, getting up and heading to the dead box.

The last player on the Sharks ran around the area, ducking behind bushes and trees, trying to find his last opponent. Two minutes passed by. Then two more.

Quinton could see that the other player was frustrated. Usually, when there were only two players left, they both hunted for each other and didn't take so long to find one another. The player's movements began to slow down. He wasn't sprinting from tree to tree anymore. After looping the entire playing field, he was back to where he started, about 20 feet from where Adam was still hiding, quiet and perfectly still.

The last remaining member of the Sharks looked back at his teammates in the dead box and lifted both his hands in a shrug. At that moment, a paintball hit him on his left hip. Adam stood up to the sound of boisterous cheers.

The Dragons were going to the championship round!

CHAPTER 8

GAME FACES

The Dragons swarmed again, but this time they swarmed Adam. They cheered and patted him on the shoulders.

"Nice shooting!"

"That was awesome!"

Logan picked up Adam and swung him around. "Little bro wins it big time!"

Quinton watched them all cheering for Adam. For a split second he was jealous, but then it dawned on him — he had been wrong. Adam was a part of his team. And this strategy was the right move for being short one person.

Quinton walked over to Adam and stopped in front of him. Adam's face looked the tiniest bit afraid, like he thought Quinton would yell at him for playing the way he did. But Quinton broke out into a huge grin. He slapped Adam on the back. "Way to go, kid!"

Adam smiled back, his happiness radiating. He gave Quinton a proud look. "I told you I wouldn't let you down."

"You did more than that. You won the whole game!" Quinton said.

Ethan and Danny high fived Adam, and then Quinton, and Logan slapped Quinton on the back. All of them practically bounced back to the common area where the announcements were made.

"You've probably figured this out," Bob said, "but the Dragons win the match 5–4. And Adam from the Dragons had two marks, putting him at a total of four, which means Quinton and Adam are tied for the MVP award with one match yet to play. Zach has three marks so far. Those are the score leaders. Up next, Zach's Bunker Busters take on the Shooting Stars. Match starts in fifteen minutes."

"Oh, man, did you hear that? You and Adam are in the race for the MVP!" Ethan jumped up and down. "I still can't believe that match!"

"Yeah, that was pretty cool," Danny said. "Logan, you really kept your cool out there."

Logan smiled and thanked him. Quinton was thrilled that they were moving on in the tournament. And he had to admit, Logan and Adam's play had definitely clinched the match.

For a moment, he thought maybe the Dragons should try Logan's strategy for all the games. But he shook his head at the thought. It was too late now. They were headed to the big match and it was best if they stuck with what they knew.

"Don't get excited, wannabes. You're not winning the tournament or the MVP. They might as well put my name on that right now." Zach patted Adam on the head as he walked by on his way to the playing field.

Danny raised his hands as if he was holding a marker and fired an imaginary paintball at Zach's back.

"Ignore him. Great job, guys," Quinton said. "Let's get ready to watch the next match. Pay attention to their tactics, see where they hide, and anything else we can use to take down the winner in the next round. Ethan, you and I will just watch Zach, since he's the best player out there, and try to figure out if he has any weaknesses. All right?"

Everyone agreed and they moved to the starting areas to see as much they could of the next match.

At the sound of the air horn, the match started and both teams charged forward aggressively.

"They both play the same style as us," Ethan commented.

"Yeah, but look how fast Zach's team is," Logan said.

"I thought we'd be the fastest team out here, but we may not be as fast as either of these teams," Danny said.

Within seconds, the initial volley of paintballs took both teams from five players down to three.

"The Shooting Stars are careful, but they don't hide very well. They run in really straight lines, too," Adam said.

"Yeah," Logan said, "but they're fast!"

Quinton was half-listening, but his attention was mostly on Zach. *Pop, pop, pop, pop!* The same pattern over and over. "Hey Ethan, have you noticed that Zach always fires four paintballs at a time? Most players do two or three."

"Yeah, that's weird," Ethan said. "I noticed something else, too. He runs in a pattern. He's always moving forward, but he alternates direction from left-right-left right — in a zigzag pattern. That's pretty predictable."

"The trick is to hit him," said Logan. "Because, man, is he fast!"

As the match continued, Quinton remained impressed by the level of play. But no matter how they moved, the Shooting Stars couldn't hit anyone else on Zach's team. One by one, the Shooting Stars were marked, and the match belonged to Zach and his team.

At the common area minutes later, Bob made the announcement. "The championship match is set! The Dragons will face Zach's Bunker Busters at three p.m. tomorrow afternoon. The match will be followed by the pizza party, as you all know, and we'll announce the winner of the MVP Award and that $100 gift certificate! As of right now, Adam, Zach, and Quinton are all tied at four marks. It should be an interesting day!"

Quinton ran his fingers through his hair. Could they actually beat Zach's team? In a head-to-head match of swarming tactics, he wasn't sure. Maybe they really did need to do something different.

He took a deep breath. It was time to do what was best for the team.

"Hey, guys!" Quinton yelled. "I call for a meeting."

"Snack bar?" Danny asked.

"No," Quinton replied. "Let's head to our spot in the woods."

"Must be serious," Ethan said.

They gathered up their gear bags and started toward their secret meeting spot.

Since the tournament was already in the woods, they didn't have far to go. Within minutes they were all perched at their usual seats on the logs.

"So, what did you guys see in that match?" Quinton asked.

"Zach shoots and runs in patterns," Ethan offered.

"His team is good," Danny said. "Really good."

"Their playing style is the same as ours," Logan said, "so we'll have to beat them at their own game to win it."

"So what are our best strengths?" Quinton asked.

"You and Logan are pretty fast and good shooters," Ethan said, "and I think I'm pretty good, too."

"Danny is good at finding the other team's players," Logan added. "I don't know how he sees them so fast."

"And, of course," Danny said, "we have the best marksman in the game!" He gave Adam a light punch on the shoulder. Everyone laughed, but then there was an awkward silence.

"Well, Commander," said Ethan. "What's the plan?"

Quinton stood up, hoping he was making the right move. He looked at the team and saw they were all watching him, waiting for him to take the lead. What had Logan said to him? *A good commander makes the best possible use of his team's skills.* Quinton took a deep breath. "Honestly, I think Zach's team is too fast for us to take on head to head."

The team's hopeful looks faded to disbelief. Ethan and Danny shared a confused look. Adam and Logan looked uneasy.

Quinton continued, "But I think there is one way we can win. Logan, I'm turning command over to you."

"What?" Logan said. "Really? Why?"

"Because we can't beat Zach's team playing their game. We need to show them something different, and I think your plan just might work. Is everyone okay with that?"

"Yeah!" the whole team said in unison.

Logan took a deep breath and released it. "Okay, guys, we're going to need to practice. Can everyone be here at eight a.m. tomorrow? We need to turn the Dragons into spiders."

CHAPTER 9

WEAVING THE WEB

The next morning, the team was up and ready to go at their spot in the woods by eight a.m. Quinton wasn't sure he was doing the right thing but he didn't know how else to beat Zach's team. Zach played aggressively and he did it really well. Logan and Adam had proved that their spider method could work. He stood next to Danny, Ethan, and Adam and looked to Logan to lead the practice.

"Okay, this should be fun," Logan said. "The first thing we need to do is charge to one side while Adam goes the other way to find his spot. Since we already know his spot is off to the left, we'll go right. That should draw Zach's team after us. Got it?"

Each team member nodded. Logan continued to go over the concepts of his strategy, and for the rest of the morning the team practiced the different maneuvers.

They broke hard right to start and stayed together, then retreated toward Adam's hiding spot. As the morning went on, they found better and better patterns to keep from bunching up or backing themselves into corners.

By lunchtime, they had their new strategy down pat and were excited about the match. When they gathered at the common area at 2:45, the place was packed with members of every team, as well as some of their other friends who liked to show up for the grand finale of the tournament.

"Are you all ready for this?" Bob asked the crowd. "This is it! The championship match between Zach's Bunker Busters and The Dragons! This match will determine the tournament champions, who will get free admission to Splatmasters Arena for the summer, as well as the first-ever tournament MVP and winner of a $100 gift certificate to Larry's Sporting Goods and Paintball Emporium. Get your teams ready. The match starts in 15 minutes!"

The Dragons double-checked their equipment and then gathered at the starting spot. They huddled close together, keeping Adam in the back so the other team couldn't even see him. Bob took his usual spot and looked at Zach. Zach gave him a nod to signal that his team was ready. Then Bob looked over at Quinton. Quinton smiled and looked at Logan, who looked back and grinned. Logan nodded, and Bob held the air horn up in the air. With a loud blast, the game was on.

Quinton, Logan, Ethan, and Danny all charged forward for a few steps and then broke hard to the right. Adam ducked behind a tree right away. Quinton grinned as he heard the crowd gasp. No one was expecting his team to move this way.

As they moved to the right, ducking and dodging behind trees, Quinton could just faintly hear Adam as he ran to the hiding spot with the stump surrounded by bushes. Zach's team charged forward, but then veered off toward the bigger group. The sound of markers popping and paintballs splattering against trees made the woods sound like one giant popcorn machine.

In that first volley, Quinton marked one of Zach's players, but Danny took a paintball to the leg. Each team was down to four players. Quinton looked around for his teammates. This wasn't going the way he'd hoped.

Quinton saw Logan break away and start to run from tree to tree, headed back toward Adam's spot. He caught Ethan's eye and, with a quick nod, they followed Logan's lead. As they retreated, they could hear Zach's team following them.

They're gaining on us! Quinton thought. *What if they're too fast and we can't reach Adam in time?*

Then Ethan yelled out. A paintball had caught him in the back of a leg.

They were already down two players. Quinton swallowed his anxiety. He looked at Logan, who nodded. The only choice was to keep moving.

Logan and Quinton continued forward. Finally Quinton saw the stump where Adam had gone to hide.

Except Adam wasn't there.

Where was he? Their plan was shot if Adam didn't do his part. Quinton felt another pang of anxiety shoot through him, but he kept going. He had to trust his teammate.

Logan and Quinton ran from tree to tree past the stump. As their pursuers came after them, he heard one quick *pop* and then another one a few seconds later. Two of Zach's teammates yelled out, "I'm marked!"

Quinton smiled and gave a little fist pump. Adam was right where he needed to be and doing his job perfectly.

Logan broke away, hoping to lure another player out into the open. The plan worked, but not perfectly. As Logan ran from one tree to the next, one of Zach's players jumped out and fired, catching Logan in the arm with a paintball. While the shooter was exposed, Quinton fired and hit him in the arm as well. The game was moving fast. Three of the Dragons were down and four of Zach's Bunker Busters were headed to the dead box. That meant it was just Quinton and Adam against Zach.

Quinton scanned the playing field, looking for any sign of Zach, but he couldn't see him. He ran to the closest tree that was big enough to provide cover, but still didn't hear or see anything. What was Zach doing?

Suddenly, from somewhere nearby, he heard Zach yell out.

"Hey, Quinton!"

"Yeah, what?" Quinton said. Talking wasn't common during matches, but there was no rule against it.

"I know you have that little squirt hiding somewhere. I'm going to find him and put a paintball right in his back! I've already marked two. One more and that MVP is mine!"

"You'll have to get me first!" Quinton yelled back. He cautiously looked around the edge of the tree trunk. Zach was hiding behind a tree only a few feet from Adam's hiding spot, but the tree was blocking Adam's angle. Quinton would have to draw him out, even if that meant getting hit.

He didn't have a shot, but if he could get Zach to move just a little, Adam would have a clear line of sight. He trusted that Adam would hit Zach. Adam was the best marksman on his team, he had finally learned.

Quinton took a deep breath and sprinted to the left. He only made it about 15 feet before he heard four *pops* as paintballs whizzed passed him. When he got behind the next tree, he took a look at his clothes to make sure he wasn't hit. Nothing. That had been close, though.

Quinton prepared to make another break for it, but before he could move he heard one more *pop,* followed by two words.

"I'm marked!"

CHAPTER 10

DRAGON VICTORY

The blast of the air horn sounded through the woods, signaling the end of the match.

What? Quinton thought. *If the match is over and I'm not marked, that means Adam must have marked Zach. We won!*

Quinton let out a whoop and ran out from behind his tree. He saw Adam crawling out from his hiding spot. Zach was only a few feet away, shaking his head. Quinton ran over to Adam to give him a hand. By the time he got there, he could see his whole team running toward them.

"You did it!" Ethan yelled.

"*Adam* did it!" Quinton said.

"No way," said Adam. "We all did it!"

The team jumped around and took turns slapping Adam on the back for getting the final shot on Zach. After a few minutes, they walked back to the common area, now decorated with ribbons and balloons, for the final announcements. The tantalizing aroma of fresh pizzas filled the air.

Bob was already standing at the podium. "Attention! Attention! Thank you everyone for yet another great Summer Paintball Tournament! I have just a couple of announcements before we get to that delicious pizza."

Quinton looked around at the crowd of paintball teams, parents, and friends. He thought back to when he was watching that school clock tick down. This was the moment he'd been waiting for. And it was even better than he could have hoped, with his whole team sharing the glory.

"This year's tournament winner and winner of a free summer of paintball at Splatmaster's Arena is . . . the Dragons!"

The crowd cheered, clapped, and whistled.

Bob continued, "They survived their short-handed match and then won it all with a 5–3 victory over Zach's Bunker Busters in the championship match. Come on up here, guys!"

The team practically ran to the podium to get their medals. The grins on their faces said it all.

"Here you go, fellas. Nice work!" Bob said as he placed a gold medal around each of their necks. They held the medals up as the town newspaper photographer took their photo. The crowd kept cheering, and Quinton's face started hurting from all the smiling. He looked down at Zach. He was standing with his team, kicking at rocks.

"And now," Bob said, "the big news you're all waiting for: the MVP award. Tied for second place with six marks each are Zach and Quinton!"

The crowd cheered, but quickly hushed when Bob held up his hand.

"This year's winner, with an astounding seven marks in just three games, is Adam!"

The crowd roared as Adam stepped up to to the podium. Bob shook his hand and then gave him the gift certificate. A light flashed as a reporter from the local paper took their picture.

"Okay everybody, let's have some pizza!" Bob said. The whole crowd cheered again and rushed forward to get to their favorite slices. The Dragons were the only ones who stayed behind.

"Nice going, Adam!" Logan said.

"Look at you, kid! You did it!" Ethan added, slapping him on the shoulder.

One by one they congratulated Adam. Quinton even wrapped him in a bear hug, making him blush furiously. After a few minutes of checking out their new medals and recapping the victory, the team started toward the lines for the pizza.

Quinton reached out and grabbed Logan's shoulder. "Hey, hold up a sec," he said.

Logan stopped and turned. "Yeah?"

"I just want to say that I'm sorry," Quinton said. He was nervous, but wanted to be honest with his friend. "I thought you were just trying to take over the team."

"I know." Logan said. "Maybe I didn't go about it just right either. I just wanted us to win."

"Yeah. It was a really smart strategy and it ended up winning the tournament for us," Quinton said. "I should have listened to you." He smiled at Logan. "That's what good commanders do, after all." Logan smiled back. Quinton went on, "Think you have more good ideas like that for next year?"

"Maybe," Logan said, then he nodded toward the rest of the team, "but we should ask them too. I bet we're not the only ones who can put together a paintball match strategy."

"Good idea," Quinton said. He and Logan grinned at each other.

The Dragons' hard work had finally paid off. They were the tournament champions.

Quinton wondered if they'd be able to do it again next year. One thing he knew for sure was that he would definitely be better at listening to his team. And he was going to ask Adam if he could teach the team some of his marksmanship skills. He knew he wouldn't be underestimating Adam or anyone else from now on.

But for now, Quinton only had one thing to decide — pepperoni or bacon pizza? He held on to his medal and joined his team for the celebration.

ABOUT THE AUTHOR

Tyler Omoth has been a freelance writer for over 10 years. He has written over 20 nonfiction books for kids on a variety of topics. He has also had stories published by writersweekly.com, dreamquestone.com, and *The Florida Writer*. Tyler has a passion for sports, with baseball being his favorite. Tyler currently lives in sunny Florida with his wife, Mary.

GLOSSARY

air horn (AYR horn)—a loud, pressure-filled container that makes a loud sound

commander (kuh-MAN-duhr)—a leader; person in charge of a team or unit

goggles (GOG-uhlz)—special, strong glasses worn over the eyes for protection

marker (MARK-ur)—in paintball, the device used to shoot paintballs

MVP—Most Valuable Player

scrimmage (SKRIM-ij) —a game played for practice

strategy (STRAT-uh-gee)—a plan to achieve a goal

tournament (TUR-nuh-muhnt)—a competition with several teams or individuals who compete for a title or prize

woodsball (WUDZ-bawl)—a paintball game played in the woods

DISCUSSION QUESTIONS

1. Logan says to Quinton, "good commanders make the best possible use of their team's skills." Do you agree? What decisions did Quinton make to be a good commander? Were there times when you thought Quinton wasn't being as good a commander as he could be?

2. Quinton often wouldn't listen to what Logan and Adam suggested. Why didn't Logan and Adam just quit the team when things didn't go their way? Why do you think they chose to follow Quinton's lead?

3. At the end of the story, Quinton decides to run out from behind the tree even though he could have gotten marked. Why did he choose to do that? How does this make him a good commander?

WRITING PROMPTS

1. Write a paragraph about someone in your
   life who has been a good leader in some way.
   What things did he or she do that point to good
   leadership skills?

2. Pretend you're Adam. What would you write in
   a letter to Quinton?

3. Can you think of a time when you or someone
   else undervalued a teammate? Write a
   paragraph about that experience.

Over 10 million people play paintball each year worldwide.

Paintball is played in more than 100 countries, on six different continents.

Woodsball is just one variation of paintball. Players could also play:

scenario—a game that has an overarching story

capture the flag—a game where each team tries to grab the flag or flags from the other team first

speedball—a game that takes place in a smaller space with equal numbers of objects on each side that players can use for cover

And many others!

The outer shell of a paintball is made from gelatin — the same stuff in JELL-O!

Ritchie White, the winner of the first game of paintball, won without firing a shot.

The first paintball game was played on June 27, 1981.

The maximum velocity a marker can fire a paintball (and still follow nationally accepted rules) is 300 feet per second.

There is such a thing as a paint grenade.

According to the number of reported injuries, paintball is safer than football, baseball, soccer, hockey, and bowling.